/4 Days

Uncle Lemon's Spring

by Jane Yolen

illustrated by Glen Rounds

"Witchin' isn't much more than common sense," said Lettie, and she had plenty of that. But was it enough to outfox Preacher Morton and rescue her Uncle Lemon?

Old Merlie, the witchin' man, started all the trouble by finding Uncle Lemon a spring. The very next day, Preacher was after the spring, demanding the debt Uncle Lemon owed him. Uncle Lemon was into Preacher's chicken house that night, and Preacher caught him. From then on, it was all up to Lettie.

Jane Yolen shows yet another facet of her creative imagination, very much in tune with Glen Rounds' irrepressibly humorous drawings.

Uncle Lemon's Spring

Uncle Lemon's Spring

by Jane Yolen

illustrated by Glen Rounds

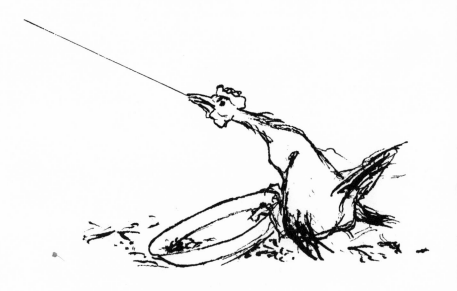

A Unicorn Book

E. P. Dutton · New York

for Adam who helped
and
for David, Bill, Dick, and Bob
who had a real Uncle Lemon

Text copyright © 1981 by Jane Yolen
Illustrations copyright © 1981 by Glen Rounds

Library of Congress Cataloging in Publication Data

Yolen, Jane.   Uncle Lemon's spring.
(A Unicorn book)
Summary: Relates how Uncle Lemon got his spring
in the middle of the driest summer on record and
the troublesome consequences it brought him.
[1. Mountain life—Fiction]
I. Rounds, Glen, date   II. Title.
PZ7.Y78Un   1981   [Fic]   80-22145
ISBN 0-525-41830-X

Published in the United States by E. P. Dutton, a Division
of Elsevier-Dutton Publishing Company, Inc., New York

Published simultaneously in Canada by Clarke,
Irwin & Company Limited, Toronto and Vancouver

Editor: Emilie McLeod   Designer: Emily Sper

Printed in the U.S.A.   First Edition
10 9 8 7 6 5 4 3 2 1

CONTENTS

ONE

———

The Witchin' Man

It was so dry that summer, the stream beds puckered up and fish practiced breathin' air. I'd lie in bed at night blessin' my Uncle Lemon for givin' me the one good window screen. He kept his window closed tight against the bugs. He *said* he mistrusted the night air, but I suspected different.

It was no wonder, then, that he woke one morning with a powerful thirst. Lord, how we needed rain. He went to the pump to get himself some water. But pump as he might, nary a drop came out.

"Dry as a popcorn fart," he said to no one in particular. " 'Bout time to *do* somethin'." So he went that very day to see Old Merlie, the witchin' man, who lives in a cave at the top of the next hill.

Old Merlie had a divinin' stick that can track down water under thirty feet of rock. You might think he'd be the first person to call on in a dry spell, but no one likes havin' truck with Merlie. Witchin' men always get somethin' from you in return.

Uncle Lemon went anyways, carryin' his walkin' stick for protection. And I followed him, quiet as a cat, through the bush.

"Old Merlie, Old Merlie," called Uncle Lemon, standin' before the cave. He dropped his walkin' stick, stood on one leg, and spat through his second and third fingers so no bad magic would fall on his head. It just about broke my heart seein' Uncle Lemon lookin' scared, 'cause he's the bravest man I know.

Suddenly there was a yawnin' and a growlin' inside the cave, and in a minute out came Old Merlie himself. He was standin' and scratchin' and lookin' like a bear just out of winter. Old Merlie had a great big black beard and long black hair that covered his head and hands and—some say, though I've never seen it—his back as well. Witchin' men always have too much of somethin', and with Old Merlie it was hair.

"Watcha' want to go and wake a man fer?" growled Old Merlie, so loud I might have fallen down with the tremblin' fears myself, if I hadn't been gazin' at Uncle Lemon standin' on his one leg and spittin' through his fingers.

Old Merlie looked at Uncle Lemon through slotted eyes, not the least bit surprised. Men standin' on one leg and spittin' through their fingers are his stock in trade.

Seein' that Old Merlie wasn't set on witchin' him right then and there, Uncle Lemon cried out, "Peace, Merlie."

Old Merlie nodded, kind of squinched up his eyes, and said "Peace" back.

So Uncle Lemon relaxed his spitter and stood down again on two feet, and I drew my first big breath and settled myself behind a pricker bush.

"I need water, Merlie," said Uncle Lemon. "Real bad."

Merlie didn't say anythin'.

"Not *real* real bad, of course," said Uncle Lemon, 'cause you don't want to give a witchin' man a hold on you. "But I've got myself a powerful thirst, and my sister Letty's child that lives with me oughta have a bath now and again."

Old Merlie unsquinched his eyes and reached back into the cave for his divinin' stick. Or maybe the stick came to him. It's hard to tell for sure with a witchin' man. Only suddenly that big old stick was there in his hairy hand, and before you could say "Uncle Lemon's Spring," Uncle Lemon and Old Merlie were off down the mountainside to localate some water.

Now I wasn't exactly hidin', just restin' behind the biggest bush I could find. I like to keep my eye on Uncle Lemon, him bein' my only blood relative in the whole world. Sometimes I keep him away from trouble, and sometimes I keep trouble away from him. It's not an easy job, neither, what with goin' to school and doin' my chores. He just naturally slips away every now and then. But summers I can usually keep ahead of him—or behind—whichever is most natural.

When he and Merlie went past me, I lost so much time standin' on one foot and spittin' through my fingers, they were clear down to the bottom before I caught up again. I could hear my heart pit-patterin' all the way down, and it was so hot and I was breathin' so hard, I didn't really figure out ahead of time where the two of them were headin'.

I caught up with them just when they turned into our very own farmyard and went right over to the pump. And didn't I feel dumb. I could have saved myself that whole trip up the mountain. And the tremblin' fears. I could have even made the house tidy like my mammy used to, just to please Uncle Lemon.

I didn't have much time for regrets though, because Old Merlie had aholt of that stick and it was out in front of him just like he was drivin' it. Only it was pullin' him and shakin' him like a tree in a big wind.

"Go to, Merlie," Uncle Lemon shouted, waving his own stick over his head. He had every bit of his courage back, now he was on home ground. I felt a lot better, too, 'cause no witchin' man can harm you when you're surrounded by your own things. "Go to, Merlie," Uncle Lemon shouted again.

Merlie paid him no mind because he was shakin' and twistin' and jumpin' like a trout on a worm. Then all of a sudden that stick stopped, and Merlie stopped too. The stick dove to the ground, and Merlie stood stock starin' still and stiff like he had died standin' up. Then he opened his mouth and said just one word: *"Dig!"*

My knees collapsed at that word, and I sat down hard on the ground.

"Girl," called Uncle Lemon, 'cause he never uses my name, "girl, stop sneakin' around and get me that shovel."

He had known I was there all along, and wasn't that just like Uncle Lemon. I knew enough to jump when his voice sounded like that. I might be scared of Merlie, but it was Uncle Lemon I had to live with. So I just ran to the shed and got out the shovel and, without bein' asked, I commenced to dig.

I must have dug five minutes before either of them said anythin' more. The dirt in our yard was hard as bone and dry as dust. I dug and dug. The further I dug, the hotter and drier I got.

Finally Merlie grunted, and Uncle Lemon reached over and grabbed the shovel from my hand. "Here, girl," he said. "You let me do that awhile. I'll show you a man's strength." And he set to.

I couldn't see he was doin' all that much better than me, only puffin' louder. Maybe after the eightieth or ninetieth shovelful Old Merlie grunted again. Uncle Lemon put both hands on the edge of the hole to haul himself up, and pulled. He pulled just in time. Merlie let out one more grunt, and that pit commenced spoutin'.

A stream of purely ice-cold crystal-clear blue-white mountain water went straight up into the air. Fifteen feet high it went without a stop, carrying the shovel with it. Light as a feather bed, the stream turned itself over and over in a sparkle of rainbows. The shovel danced on top of the water to the sound of the stream.

Then Old Merlie pounded once on the ground with his stick, and the spring stopped singing and started down.

Uncle Lemon caught the shovel as it fell, stepped under the water, and opened his mouth. The drops splattered down into it till he was all full up.

"Thank-ee, Merlie," said Uncle Lemon. "That was purely good."

Uncle Lemon didn't notice me under the stream,

gettin' filled up too. Or gettin' a pail of water for our brindle cow, our big old steer, and the mule. He just went over to the chicken coop and got out our last hen. She wasn't good for much, that hen. She hadn't laid an egg in over a year. But I kept hopin'.

Merlie didn't say anythin'. He just tucked that hen under his arm and went straightaway up the mountain and back into his cave.

And that's how Uncle Lemon got his spring in the middle of the driest summer on record. And how we both got trouble.

TWO

———

Preacher Morton

Wasn't a day, maybe two, before word got down to the valley that we had water. I carried bottles of it to families that were hardest off and they told their neighbors and friends. With one thing and another, we got a visit from that travelin' man of God, Preacher Morton.

Lord, how I despised that man. He used to be a junkman and the fattest person in these parts. One day he found God and lost weight. Now he's skinny as a turkey vulture and twice as homely.

It wasn't his looks that bothered me. After all, Uncle Lemon's no prize, and pretty faces don't rightly run in our family. Preacher drove my mammy off our farm. It wasn't more than a hardscrabble place at best, but he took it, and she died of a broken heart. So it's no wonder I hate him.

We weren't especially surprised when he came

callin'. Around our parts water means money. And Preacher's so almighty took up with God and money that he keeps the Sabbath and everythin' else he can get his hands on. Includin' other folks' properties.

Preacher still walks like a fat man. His skinny body carries the ghost of all that weight. Most days you can hear him laboring up the mountainside. But what with Uncle Lemon's spring burblin' and singin' into its catch hole, I didn't hear Preacher till he was there.

"Peace, friends," came his deep, wheezy voice. "I've come to bless your spring."

That's when I *knew* we had trouble.

"Peace, friends," Preacher Morton said again, figurin' what sounds good once sounds better twice. "Friends," said Preacher, "for five dollars, only five dollars, I will bless this spring. Make it good, I said good, for all eternity."

"Now why don't you bless yourself back down the hill?" said Uncle Lemon, only barely on this side of good manners. "We don't need any blessing. It's a blessing that this spring came out at all. It blesses itself with every bubble it makes."

I thought that was real pretty and almost said so, only I could never talk to Uncle Lemon like that. He might laugh, or worse, he might not say anythin' at all.

The spring talked for me. It raised itself back up about five feet and sang its own blessing, a-poppin' and burblin' and gigglin' and gurglin' for a minute before it settled back down again.

Preacher never noticed the spring song, for he was much too busy sellin' salvation. "Nothin' is blessed without a blessin' from a preacher," he said, holdin' up a thick black imitation-leather Bible as if to strike Uncle Lemon with it. "You are a sinner, a sinner, Lemon Cleary, thinkin' that way."

I stepped back a bit, nerves risin' inside of me like wires sparkin'. You *never* speak to Uncle Lemon like

that or raise your hand to him, 'less you're lookin' for a bruise. Many a man and a mountain cat has found that out too late.

"Sinner I may be," roared Uncle Lemon, forgettin' which side of his manners he was on, "but on my own property I sin any way I like."

He reached over with one of his big, hard-knuckled hands and grabbed the front of Preacher's ruffled white shirt. He left dirty fingerprints on it big as knotholes. Preacher's string tie shook so hard underneath Uncle Lemon's hands, it looked like the legs of a saved soul at prayer meetin'. Took some of Preacher's wind away, too, I can tell you. After whackin' away at Uncle Lemon with both hands and his Bible, Preacher knocked himself free, backed away a step or three, slipped and fell, bottom down. The dust had become a pool of mud because of the spring. It sucked up Preacher's rear like a hog in a wallow.

I laughed out loud. That was a mistake. Lord, I wish I could rein in my sense of humor.

"*Your* property!" yelled Preacher Morton up at us. "*Your* property, is it? I'd like to remind you that I hold a note, a note I say, on this land. And if I don't get my five dollars or . . ." and here he paused. His eyes rolled up in his head and his tongue made circles around the outside of his mouth. Suddenly I recollected what Uncle Lemon had said—that Preacher's brain is mostly connected with his stomach. I might have started to laugh again except Preacher's voice continued, coming at us out of the mud. "Yessir, five dollars or one of your fine fat settin' hens better find its way down to my place by tomorrow midday latest. If I don't get one or t'other, I might just call due that note. And I'll run you off this property, this very property, just like I ran your sister off hers. And her property wasn't worth diddly compared to this, now that it's got such an almighty clear-lookin' *unblessed* spring."

His words made a cold sweat run down my back-bone. I started to shake, both from his words and what I was afraid Uncle Lemon might do. Uncle Lemon has had a passel of problems with the law before, and I sure didn't want anythin' to happen to Uncle Lemon.

My sweat was cold, but it was warm compared to Uncle Lemon's voice. *It* got icy and low and hard and came out of his mouth in little steel pellets. "Just you get out of here. Now. You'll get *your* chicken or my name ain't Lemon Clarkson Cleary."

Preacher backed away from those words like they was comin' out of a shotgun. He backed away, pushing

through the mud, but he smiled. He thought he held power over Uncle Lemon, what with his imitation-leather Bible, and his note on the property, and especially now that he knew Uncle Lemon's true name. Preacher smiled like a rattler smiles, all lips and no teeth. Then he picked himself up and went back down the hill. He was puffin' harder than when he came up, and he was a whole lot dirtier.

Uncle Lemon turned and looked at me with half a grin. "Girl," he said, spittin' to one side, "Hell is so full of preachers, you can see their feet stickin' out the windows."

I nodded, but I had somethin' to say and was goin' to bust if I didn't get it said. "Uncle Lemon," I said, "you gave the last of our hens to Merlie."

Uncle Lemon put his head to one side. "I recollect," he said slowly, as if he had just thought of it himself, "that I gave the last of my settin' hens to Merlie. And she hadn't laid an egg in over a year."

It was his way of sayin' thanks for the reminder. The way he feels about most talk is that people let their tongues wag like the south end of a northbound goose.

I nodded again.

Uncle Lemon went on. "So we haven't got a hen to give Preacher."

I nodded again.

"Only have that brindle cow that gives milk every third month, and that six-year-old steer you went and gave a name to when you were too young to know better so now I can't slaughter it."

"I'm sorry," I said, lookin' down at the ground, but I wasn't really. I loved Bully, our old steer. He followed me around like a dog.

"Of course," he added, "there's always that durn-fool mule."

That mule had kicked me so often, I'd have loved to give it away. I rubbed my backside. It still ached with the memory of that mule's feet. But I wouldn't want to give even *that* mule to Preacher Morton.

"Not to Preacher Morton," I begged.

That surprised Uncle Lemon. He stared at me a moment and I raised my chin up to show him that beggin' didn't necessarily mean I was afraid. If I didn't know better, I'd have to say his eyes was mistin' a bit. That happens sometimes, when he thinks of my mammy. She raised him up just like he was doin' for me.

"But Uncle Lemon," I said at last, "what'll we do?"

"*We?*" said Uncle Lemon. He squatted down in the dirt to think.

"We!" I said, hunkerin' down with him. I began to draw a slow line in the mud, with my finger.

Then, just as slowly, Uncle Lemon pulled out an idea from behind his teeth. "Preacher's got hens."

"Uncle Lemon . . ."

"Mighty plump hens, too, I recollect."

"Uncle Lemon!" I breathed.

"And some of them was once mine."

"Most of them was," I added in a hurry. "Most of them was ours—before Preacher Morton took them."

"So they were," said Uncle Lemon.

I looked at him and he looked at me. And that's when we planned on fishin' for chickens.

THREE

Fishin' for Chickens

It was half past sunrise when we lit out down the road. Uncle Lemon was in front with his walkin' stick and me behind with my heart somewhere up the side of my throat. I was so blamed scared, my tongue went rattlin' along like a clatterbone.

"Are you sure you know what we're doin'? Uncle Lemon?"

Silence.

"We're goin' to get in a mess of trouble, Uncle Lemon."

Thwack went the stick against an aspen and the leaves commenced to tremblin' and chatterin'.

"Don't you think this is a mite dangerous, Uncle Lemon?"

"*Girl,* what have I told you about jawin'?"

I was still.

So we trotted through the half-light on down the road that twisted like a big old cottonmouth. Tree shadows kept makin' new patches on the road. Even my thoughts scared me and I wished Uncle Lemon would let me talk them away.

At last we came to Preacher Morton's place. It's the best bottomland on Back Fork, spreadin' out low and clean with nary a bump or hillock on it. It can grow just about anythin': taters, corn, greens, even tobacco. The barn is covered with signs: Chew Mail Pouch Tobacco. Drink Coca-Cola. Jesus Saves.

And it was quiet, too quiet by half for me. There weren't any cats howlin', birds peepin', hogs snufflin', cows lowin'. Even the rooster wasn't up. Every step Uncle Lemon took sounded *KABLOOM,* that loud. My steps weren't much quieter.

We crept up to a thicket right by the chicken house. Uncle Lemon hunkered down and I was right beside him.

I watched him take a mess of string out of his overalls pocket. Then he took out a handful of corn. Next he took his knife from his back pocket and made a wee bitty hole in two pieces of corn and ever so slowly poked the string through, tyin' a knot on t'other side. He tied the one end of the string onto his walkin' stick and gave a satisfied grunt that echoed all through the thicket.

By now, day was all around us and it seemed so light, we fair shimmered in that thicket. But inside the chicken house it was still as black as God's pocket.

Uncle Lemon got down on his knees and crawled slower than slow to the fence, keepin' the chicken house between him and Preacher's door. Me, I stayed in the thicket, gathered up the rest of the corn and put it in my overalls pocket. Didn't want any evidence left. And all the while my knees were makin' body music, one against the other, I was *that* scared.

Uncle Lemon didn't seem scared, though. He tossed the string up over the fence not far from the henhouse door.

I held my breath as he slowly pulled the string back towards him. There was a rustlin' from inside, but the hens stayed put.

Uncle Lemon pulled the string back over the fence and tried again. This time the corn hit the henhouse

doorframe and dropped down onto the stoop. There was a cluckin' inside as if the hens were makin' up their minds—or their beds—but none of them came to the door to check it out. Uncle Lemon pulled the line back over the fence with a jerk.

"Dang-blamed line," he muttered, so loud I could hear every syllable. "Dang-blamed chickens. Dang-blamed chicken house."

Then he suddenly stood up like he was in a good hole on Back Fork openin' day of fishin' season. He drew his hand back and cast that corn perfectly, right through the door of the chicken house.

"Got ya!" he called out with a mule's laugh. And he dragged out a mighty surprised-lookin' hen with her beak clamped tight on the string and the corn already halfway down her gullet.

Before I had time to make a sound, there was a sudden movement close to Uncle Lemon's side. I heard a real loud click—a hammer drawn back on a shotgun.

"I caught ya, ya hen-hustlin' heathen!" It was Preacher Morton. He was too excited to repeat himself.

I flattened myself deeper into the thicket and shoved my hand against my mouth so as not to make a sound. I watched as Preacher pushed Uncle Lemon with the barrel of his gun. They marched off towards Preacher's

house and disappeared. Preacher was so intent on keepin' Uncle Lemon in front of that gun, he never noticed me at all. I tippytoed out after them and peeked through a convenient window. Old Preacher was shoving Uncle Lemon down in his root cellar. He locked the door and pushed a chair up under the handle. No matter how Uncle Lemon called out and cursed and shook the knob, the chair held.

"I'm gonna call the sheriff now, Lemon Clarkson Cleary," said Preacher Morton with his rattler's smile. "You know he's the meanest, most quarrelsome man in the county. And *you're* goin' to stay nice and cool down that cellar, while I do."

Then he went to ring the operator, quick as summer lightnin'. But Sheriff must have been out or not answerin' because Preacher slammed the phone down and said some mighty unchristian words. He shook his fist at the phone and then at the root cellar. Then he settled himself down for some serious eatin'. I went back to the thicket.

I allowed myself five minutes to whimper and five minutes to shake, then made up my mind. " 'Bout time to *do* somethin'," I said quietly in a voice I hoped sounded like Uncle Lemon's. And that's when I went up the mountain to talk with Old Merlie.

FOUR

To the Rescue

EVERY STEP UP TO Old Merlie's cave I drug my feet. I felt like I was belly-deep in cold water and the river was risin'. After all, I had never talked to Old Merlie myself and wasn't sure what to say. Besides, I didn't have a chicken to give him, just the dry brindle cow, six-year-old Bully, and that durn-fool mule. And they were really Uncle Lemon's, not mine. Everythin' I had was really Uncle Lemon's. When my mammy died, she left everythin' to Uncle Lemon, and her everythin' was me. So I had nothin' of my own, really. And you can't give what you don't own to a witchin' man. It makes the magic go all peculiar.

But I finally got up to that cave because I *had* to.

"Old Merlie," I shouted out, the sound makin' it after three tries. Even then it was more like a bullfrog on a summer night, all croak.

I stood on my left leg and spat through my second and third fingers. "Old . . . (*spit spit*) Merlie (*spat spat*)," I called again. I was between *spits* and *spats* when he came out.

"You done it agin," he said. "Wakin' a man up from his hiber-a-nation." He said it like it was some kind of country.

"Peace, Merlie," I called out, just like Uncle Lemon.

Merlie growled twice, scratched himself under the arm and started back into his cave. "Kids," he said and spat to one side. I swear smoke came up where he spat.

"Please, Mr. Merlie . . ." I said. And I came down off that one leg and ran up to him. I grabbed aholt of his hand. It was a horny hand, calloused and cold for all that its back was covered with hair.

"Kids," Merlie said again when I touched him, and he turned to look at me, his eyes squinched down some.

I suddenly remembered who he was and managed to get back on my one leg and raise my fingers and pucker my spitter and squeak out, "Peace, Merlie."

"Oh, peace yerself," he said, gentle-like. Then he added, "Peace, little Letty." And it took me a moment to remember that was my name as well as my mammy's because Uncle Lemon only calls me *girl*.

And then I had to tell him about Preacher Morton and blessin' the spring and the five dollars and fishin' for chickens and all the rest. He slapped his knee and opened his mouth, and the strangest sound came out. It was a laugh, I'm sure. It started down real low like this:

ARH HRH HRH

and then went about middle high like this:

HEHEHEHEHEHEHEHEHEHEHEHEHEHEHEHE

and then plumb jumped a mile to a cackle like this:

YAA-HAA-HAA   YAA-HAA-HAA

and then it stopped.

"I'm tired," he said.

"But what about Uncle Lemon?"

"I'm tired, little Letty," he said.

"But what about Uncle Lemon?" I'm nothin' if not bullheaded.

Then Old Merlie drew himself up, taller than anyone I ever did see. "You know what you can do about Lemon Wilber Cleary," he said, usin' Uncle Lemon's *real* name. Not the fake one palmed off on Preacher.

"But I don't," I screeched.

And then he began singin' in his cracky old voice:

> Fox in the henhouse
> Listen to him sing;
> Out come the preacher
> Catch him in the spring.

When he finished, he turned and went back into his cave. That was all!

I didn't dare follow. I sat down by the cave and commenced cryin'. Not soppy little-girl tears, the kind Uncle Lemon hates, but big man-gasping sobs. They just heaved out of me like a bull roar.

And then all of a sudden I stopped. It came to me just like that. I *did* know what to do about Uncle Lemon. Old Merlie knew I knew, too. And for good measure, he had told me what to do—plain as plain.

If I hadn't been such a sobbin' fool, I'd have understood right off.

Fox in the henhouse indeed. Why, witchin' isn't much more than common sense. Common sense and no tears.

So I headed down the mountainside to outfox Preacher Morton.

FIVE

Fox Among the Chickens

I NEEDED DARK. So it was past supper and headin' into sundown when I went back to Preacher's. Not that I had eaten much. My stomach had been jumpin' all day like a sack of hoptoads.

I crept over to the henhouse thicket and waited for the sun to set. It was still hot enough to melt lard on a roof, but I felt cold. Colder than a mine shaft. Colder than Uncle Lemon's spring.

The light went on at Preacher's. I could see into his kitchen and danged if that man wasn't still eatin' and jawin' at the root cellar. I was so far away, I couldn't make out more'n a mumble.

But soon it got to be real dark, and I began to make some rustlin' sounds by the chicken house. Not much, but enough to make Preacher nervous. I went back and checked through the window. Preacher stood up, looked about, put his hand to his ear, sat back down again.

Then I headed off a ways up the mountain and barked like a fox. Wouldn't have fooled a fox. Wouldn't have fooled a dog either, but Preacher didn't hold with dogs. He had been bitten so often as a junk-man that even as a preacher he was still scared. That bark of mine wouldn't have fooled Uncle Lemon, but it sure enough fooled old Preacher. He stepped to the

doorway with his shotgun in his hand and the light behind him lit him up for all the world to see. He looked around, listened real hard, then went back in and closed the door.

I let him get settled down again. About an hour later, the lights went off in his house, and I figured he had gone to bed. Then I sneaked, quieter than any fox, over to the chicken house. Suddenly I stubbed my toe on somethin' and had to grab aholt of my mouth to keep from cryin' out. When I bent down to see what I had stumbled on, danged if it wasn't Uncle Lemon's stick with the string still tied to it. It was just what I needed.

When my toe stopped smartin', I leaned over the fence and aimed the walkin' stick into the henhouse as best I could, seein' there wasn't any light. I just pre-

tended I was out on Back Fork fishin' with Uncle
Lemon, and let go of the stick. But I held fast to the
string.

It went right into the coop. I yanked on the string
and that stick rattled around the henhouse and stirred
those setters something fierce. Then I hauled out the
stick by the string, in the fastest hand-over-hand you
ever did see, and ran straight off to the far side of
Preacher's house.

He was up and out in record time, with his hair and
nightshirt so messed, he looked like he'd been chawin'
tobacco and spittin' against the wind. He had grabbed
up his shotgun and he came out shootin', *blamity-blam,*
with only the porch light to guide him. Only thing that
saved his chickens was that they were still in the henhouse.

He stopped shootin' for a minute to look around for the fox. By that time I was far up the mountain path. Out of sight of the house, I commenced barkin' again.

Preacher started up the path after me and when he got close enough, I hauled off and threw Uncle Lemon's walkin' stick as far as ever I could into the briars. I heard it tumble and crackle and snap things as it fell down the mountainside. Last I could make out, Preacher headed into the brush after that stick, still thinkin' it was a fox.

I scooted back down the path and around to Preacher's front door. I went in and yanked the chair out from under the root cellar doorknob, callin' as I did it, "Uncle Lemon, Uncle Lemon, come out quick."

All I heard was a snore.

I couldn't believe it. Uncle Lemon was asleep. I was so angry, I made it down the stairs in the dark and shook him.

"Girl, what're you doin' here?" was all he could say.

"Just set your feet towards home," I said. "And when you think of it, you might say thanks." Then I ran up the stairs and out the door.

Well, at first Uncle Lemon was right behind me and then of a sudden he wasn't. I was so mad and scared I almost didn't care. Then I heard some smashin' and crashin' and squawkin' sounds out by the chicken house.

"O Lord," I said, in a hasty got-together prayer, "don't let Preacher catch him now. Preacher will shoot first and look after."

Then I heard the crashin' close by me. "Don't let it be Preacher," I prayed out loud. "Lord, a load of birdshot can hurt me a lot worse than it can hurt a tough old hide like Uncle Lemon's."

I looked back and something was gainin' on me, something tall as a man and shadow thin. It had two legs and a head and a big lump where one of its arms should be. And if I hadn't promised myself to give up cryin' and screamin', I would have opened my mouth right there.

"Girl, let's go." That shadow was Uncle Lemon. And when he came closer, I made out under his arms one of the fattest settin' hens I ever did see.

"This one's for the preacher," he said. "Payment for blessin' our spring."

SIX

Preacher Goes A-huntin'

IT DIDN'T TAKE PREACHER more than four or five hours to put it all together. Preacher's not dumb, he's just mean.

But he couldn't labor up the hill without huffin' and puffin'. So even in our sleep and even with the spring burblin' in its catch hole, our ears gave us warnin'.

Uncle Lemon woke first. He had already gotten himself lots of sleep in the root cellar.

I was a mite slower.

"Girl," he said, comin' into my room, "we got company."

I put my feet on the floor. I had fallen asleep in my clothes so there wasn't all that much to gettin' up. Even with my eyes closed and my ears half-asleep, I could tell it was Preacher.

To make me feel better, I sang Merlie's song:

Fox in the henhouse
Listen to him sing;
Out come the preacher
Catch him in the spring.

"That's it, girl," said Uncle Lemon. "We'll surely catch him now. Go up and get the garbage can lid. Tie it to a nice long length of clothesline. Then go put it down bang-hard on the spring. Sit on it till I come for you."

That sounded plain silly and I had gotten brave enough to say so. "That'll hold down the spring water. It'll build up under me somethin' fierce."

"Do as I say," was all Uncle Lemon said.

I did it, too, quicker than quick. Got the lid and tied the rope and slammed it on top of the spring. Then I sat down on the lid. And all the while I could hear the spring gettin' angrier and angrier right under me, tryin' to push me up. It wouldn't have taken too much pushin', either. I only weigh about eighty-nine pounds.

Just then Uncle Lemon shoved his still and wood stove out of the house, right over to where I was sittin'. I moved over on the lid a tad, and he pushed them right up against me. They weigh about four hundred pounds.

"Now, girl, you ease off altogether," said Uncle Lemon.

I did, and he shoved the still and wood stove on top of the spring.

"Pick up the rope and go over by the chicken coop." And I did.

"When I holler," said Uncle Lemon, "pull for all you're worth."

"What are you gonna holler?" I asked and hoped I wasn't too sleepy to remember.

"Don't rightly know yet," said Uncle Lemon, "but I expect you'll recognize it when you hear it."

So I was waitin' up on top of the henhouse when Preacher appeared. He looked like an accident on its way to happen. He still had on his nightshirt, tucked into the top of his pants. He had on shoes but no socks. His hands and feet were scratched and bleedin'. In his hands was Uncle Lemon's walkin' stick with the string still attached. Danged if he wasn't mad.

Sheriff was with him, lookin' big and mean, with a zigzag scar under one eye and a red moustache that droops on both sides of his mouth. He always wears a gun. Even in his sleep, or so I've heard tell. But he chews gum instead of tobacco.

Uncle Lemon was perched up on top of his wood stove, carvin' a new walkin' stick, and whistlin' "Bear Creek Sally Goodin."

"Mornin' Cousin Lemon," said Sheriff. He's kin to most folk around here.

"Mornin', FJ," said Uncle Lemon.

Preacher didn't say anythin'. And I was mum as a china-head doll.

"Heard you was in a little scuffle at Preacher's," said Sheriff.

Uncle Lemon crossed his arms. "First I was told of it."

"Took a chicken, so I hear," said Sheriff.

"Now, who'd you hear that from, FJ?" asked Uncle Lemon.

Sheriff looked over at Preacher and was quiet. All I could hear was his gum crackin' and the stream cursin' down there in its hole.

" 'Course I know you don't need any hens, havin' your own setters," said Sheriff.

"Don't need none when you have some," agreed Uncle Lemon. "That's what my dear sister Letty used to say, bless her."

"If I heard you needed one, I might believe you took one," said Sheriff, fingerin' his gun.

"And you'd be right, FJ," said Uncle Lemon. Uncle Lemon didn't hold with lying. And through that entire conversation, he didn't tell a *direct* lie. Not once.

I might have turned a funny color right about then. But Sheriff never noticed. Instead he turned to Preacher who was standin' there holdin' on to that old walkin' stick for all it was worth.

"Now, Lemon Cleary never lies," said Sheriff. "That's a well-known truth. So I'm gonna ask you direct. Why would he want one of *your* hens?"

"He owed me," said Preacher.

"What for?" asked Uncle Lemon, easy and fast, like a strikin' snake.

Preacher didn't answer that one. He looked at the stick, then down at the ground, over to me sittin' on the henhouse, then back again at Uncle Lemon. But he couldn't say what for, because blessin' springs wasn't a legal matter. And the way he wanted to bless it wasn't right besides. He kind of spluttered and let out a breath and flung the stick angrily at the henhouse.

The stick hit the door, and the fat settin' hen inside squawked angrily, got off her nest, ran out the door, and raced off down the mountain path.

Sheriff let out a small chuckle, patted the gun in his belt, turned on his heel, and went down the hill after her. "Good to see you, Lemon," he called as he went. "You and the girl stop in for some of Betty Lee's rhubarb pie real soon." He didn't look back.

Uncle Lemon grunted.

I commenced to laugh. It wasn't much of a laugh, really, just a small giggle, but it was enough to make Preacher angry.

It made him so mad, he commenced wavin' his arms and yellin' out "You made me, made me tell a lie. And that's against the will of the Lord."

"What makes you think you're doin' the Lord's work?" asked Uncle Lemon. "Why, Preacher, you never did know beans from birds' eggs."

I had to put my word in too. "It wasn't any worse than the lie you told us about havin' to bless the spring."

"*The spring!* Why, what have you done with that spring?" Preacher asked suddenly, his head goin' around on his neck like an owl after supper. "It's the only gusher in the county."

"I'm settin' on it, Preacher," said Uncle Lemon, gettin' up slow and easy. "A man has a right to set on his own property."

"It's not goin' to be your property for long, Lemon Cleary. It's goin' to be *my* property. And *my* spring," said Preacher, his eyes glazed over with greed. "I could sell water at a dollar a bottle in drought times. At two dollars a bottle. At ten . . ."

Uncle Lemon moved a tad further from the wood stove. "Well, Preacher," he said, "I've been thinkin' of puttin' that spring back down under the ground where it rightly belongs. Got it from a witchin' man, after all. And no Christian soul would want to take anythin' from a witchin' man."

"You move all that stuff off'n *my* spring," said Preacher, so tremblin' with the gimmes, he had mixed up *his* and *ours* for good. "You got no right to plug it."

"Move it yourself," said Uncle Lemon, and he walked back towards the house.

Old Preacher didn't take a minute to do any thinkin'. He just did a whole lot of pushin'. He puffed and he shoved till he had moved the still and the stove off the spring hole. Then he bent down to pull off the lid, which had gotten scrunched down into the mud on both sides of the spring.

As Preacher bent over, Uncle Lemon turned around and yelled, "Let her blow, Letty."

I was so surprised he used my name that I fell backwards off the henhouse, pullin' the rope as I went, and the lid ripped right off of the spring.

SEVEN

Leftover Chicken

WHEN THE COVER CAME rippin' off that spring hole, the water blew. The ground spouted just like a whale, and Preacher was carried up off his feet easier than the shovel. He turned over and over and over on the top of that spout, 'bout twenty feet off the ground. He must have been wet clean through to his gizzard, and scared, too, hangin' up there so high.

"Let me down," he hollered.

And I commenced to laugh.

"Well, what do you think, Letty?" asked Uncle Lemon, once we'd stopped hee-hawin'. "Do you trust him?"

I tried to look serious and that started us laughin' all over again.

"I don't trust him either," said Uncle Lemon at last. "Even up in that water saddle." And then, because

Preacher couldn't hear us over the roar of the spout, Uncle Lemon shouted, "WE DON'T TRUST YOU!"

"I SWEAR," Preacher yelled and sputtered, "I SWEAR ON MY MAMMY'S GRAVE NOT TO BOTHER YOU AGAIN."

Uncle Lemon chewed on that a bit. Then he shouted back, "DO YOU MEAN ABOUT THE SPRING OR ABOUT THE CHICKENS?"

Preacher turned over in the water again and was facedown, hanging dangerously over the side. "ABOUT EITHER," he called.

"DONE!" Uncle Lemon shouted back and nodded so Preacher would be sure to understand.

Then we pushed our stove over to the spring spout. The mud was now up to our knees. It was hard goin' but we laughed all the way. The stove was heavy enough to cut the gusher in half. Preacher came down all in a heap, *Bang!* just like that.

He was bruised a bit and splattered a lot more, but he had promised on his Mammy's grave, and even Preacher knew better than to go back on that. So he had to leave us be. He just picked himself up from the ground and, without even a by-your-leave, stumbled home.

No sooner had he gone round a bend than, with a faint murmur, the spring stopped tryin' to spout and commenced burblin' again. So we shoved the stove to one side and sat down on it.

"If Preacher had waited, he wouldn't have had to swear," I said.

"If pigs had wings, they'd build nests in trees," said Uncle Lemon. "Preacher never was one for waitin'." Then he winked at me and put his arm around my shoulder.

"Well, you have your spring back," I said.

"*Our* spring, little Letty," said Uncle Lemon.

I looked at him, not knowing what to say.

"When I saw you sittin' so serious up atop that chicken house," said Uncle Lemon, "with your little pointed chin set so determined, you 'minded me of your mammy."

"So *that's* why you called me Letty," I said.

Uncle Lemon stood down from the stove. He wiped his arm across his eyes, 'cause he must have been fair perspirin' from the heat. "I called you Letty cause that's your name, girl. And it's high time you learned it. Now, we'd better get this stuff back into the house."

He started shovin' before I could get down, and continued to jaw at me. "Your mammy raised me up to be as strong as a man and as lovin' as a woman. I've tried to raise you up that same way, but you're learnin' better than I ever did."

I hopped down and started shovin' alongside of him. "I think you've done just fine, Uncle Lemon," I said, but I said it real quiet-like so he could pretend he didn't hear.

Then I had a worrisome thought. "Uncle Lemon," I said, "Remember, it was Old Merlie told me how to get you from the root cellar. It was Old Merlie who said we ought to catch Preacher in the spring. Only I didn't give him anythin' for it 'cause I had nothing to give. You know you can't give a witchin' man what isn't rightly yours."

Uncle Lemon said nothin', but went over to the henhouse where the hen had been settin'. She wasn't back yet, probably still cowerin' down the hill.

"Well, looky here," said Uncle Lemon. He came back out of the henhouse holdin' a beautiful new-laid egg in his hand. He handed it to me, real gentle-like. "This egg is *yours*," he said. "We'd never have got it without you."

"*Ours*. It's *ours,* Uncle Lemon," I answered.

He smiled. "Ours," he said. "Now you take it on up to Old Merlie. And don't you forget your thank-ees. There are *some* things I taught you."

And that's when I commenced walkin' back, egg in hand, to the cave on top of the mountain. I wasn't scared at all, not one little bit, but just in case, I whistled "Bear Creek Sally Goodin" just as loud as ever I could, just like Uncle Lemon.